THE RIDDLE

RETOLD BY ADELE VERNON ◂ ILLUSTRATED BY
ROBERT RAYEVSKY AND VLADIMIR RADUNSKY

BASED ON AN OLD CATALAN STORY
"EL REI I EL CARBONER"
("THE KING AND THE CHARCOAL MAKER")

DODD, MEAD & COMPANY   NEW YORK

Text copyright © 1987 by Adele Vernon
Illustrations © 1987 by Robert Rayevsky and Vladimir Radunsky
Distributed in Canada by McClelland and Stewart
Limited, Toronto.
Printed in Hong Kong by South China Printing Company.
1 2 3 4 5 6 7 8 9 10
Design by Robert Rayevsky and Vladimir Radunsky
Library of Congress Cataloging-in-Publication Data
Vernon, Adele.
The riddle.
Summary: A retelling of a traditional Catalan tale
in which a poor charcoal maker's cleverness wins him an
unexpected fortune.
[1. Folklore—Spain] I. Rayevsky, Robert, ill.
II. Radunsky, Vladimir, ill. III. Title.
PZ8.1.V479Ri 1987   398.2′1′09467   87-508
ISBN 0-396-08920-8

For Mother Bear and Oral—AV

Once upon a time, long, long ago a king lost his way while hunting in a great forest. The king was cold, tired, and hungry, but there was no one around to help him.

"Oh, where are all my companions?" lamented the king. When suddenly, not far off, he noticed thin spires of smoke drifting up through the tall trees. Guided by the smoke, the king soon came to a clearing in the forest where there lived a poor charcoal maker and his family.

The charcoal maker was busily stacking wood into a mound and didn't hear the king approaching.

"Good day!" greeted the king in a booming voice.

This so startled the charcoal maker that he spun around, sending sticks of wood flying in all directions. His face and hands were covered with soot, and he stepped forward and peered at the king from beneath a mat of reddish hair.

"Ah, my good man," continued the weary king, "could you spare me a drink of water and some food? I have had no refreshment all day."

The charcoal maker, who had been looking intently at this finely dressed stranger, suddenly realized that it was THE KING who stood before him.

"Y...Your Majesty? Oh, dear! C...can it really be you?" stammered the charcoal maker, not quite believing his own eyes. "Yes, of course, Your Majesty. Please, sit down. Here, by the fire."

After making a hasty bow he called excitedly to his wife.

"Anna, Anna! Some water! Some food! Quickly! It is His Majesty, THE KING!"

In the space of a wink, a plump, ruddy-faced woman came scurrying out of the hut, balancing a plate of steaming roasted onions and carrying a jug of cold water.

"Pardon us, Your Majesty. We have so little to offer you,"

apologized Anna as she set the food down near the king. And with a flustered curtsey, she hurried back to the hut.

The king ate and drank with great gusto.

"Mmmmm, delicious! How hungry and thirsty I was. This fresh cold water is better than wine. You see, I was hunting with my companions when we got separated and I lost my way. They must have returned to the castle thinking that I had gone home."

After his meal, the king looked around at the smoking mounds and wondered about the hard life of a charcoal maker.

"And you, charcoal maker," inquired the king, motioning for him to sit down, "living here in the middle of the forest, far from village or castle, working long hours to make charcoal for others to burn and receiving little thanks for your labor, how much do you earn a day for your work?"

The charcoal maker answered the king cheerfully as he put more wood on the fire, "No more than ten cents a day, Your Majesty. And a great plenty it is too!"

"What!?" exclaimed the king, unable to hide his surprise. "You can't mean it! How can you live on so little?"

"Not only do I make enough to live on," explained the charcoal maker briskly, "but I also pay back a debt, save for my old age, and still have something left over to throw out the window!"

Amazed, the king leaned forward to look more closely at the sturdy little man sitting before him.

"But it is not possible! How can you do so much with such meagre earnings?"

"It is very simple, Your Majesty," said the charcoal maker with a twinkle in his eye.

"With my earnings I support my family which includes my mother, who took care of me when I was young. Now I am taking care of her. Thus, I am paying back a debt. I also provide for my son, whom I hope will do the same for me when I am old.

So, I am saving for my old age. Finally, I must provide a dowry for my daughter who will marry some day. And as you know, Your Majesty, money spent on a dowry is as good as throwing it out the window."

The king laughed long and hard at the charcoal maker's riddle. He was delighted with the story but now he was curious to see if such an ingenious man was also honest and trustworthy. So he made a bargain with him.

"Well, charcoal maker, I see that you are both clever and resourceful. I admire you greatly. But I ask you to keep this talk of ours a secret. Do not reveal the answer to this riddle to anyone until you have looked upon my face one hundred times. Agreed?"

The charcoal maker stood up quickly and made a deep bow.

"Yes, of course, Your Majesty. You have my word of honor."

Pleased with his bargain, the king made ready to go.

"Thank you for the delicious meal. Now I must go. Please be good enough to show me the way back to the main road."

"It has been an honor, Your Majesty," answered the charcoal maker, bowing again. "Please come this way."

The next day in the great dining hall of the castle, the king feasted and jested with the members of his court. After the huge meal, he challenged them with the charcoal-maker's riddle.

"Now tell me, can any of you solve this riddle? How can a poor charcoal maker, who earns only ten cents a day, make enough to live on, pay back a debt, save for his old age, and even have something left over to throw out the window? Whoever is the first with the answer shall be made First Counsellor of the Kingdom."

Immediately the hall was filled with a great hum-buzz as wisemen, courtiers, and scholars talked about the riddle. Many attempted to solve it, but the king, his eyes shining with delight, shook his head—No!—again and again. No one in the whole court could find the answer.

Only one courtier did not participate in the debate. He quietly got up from the table, tied a bag to his belt, and with a cunning smile, slipped out of the palace unnoticed.

After a long ride, he approached the charcoal maker's home.

"I say, you there, charcoal maker," called out the courtier, "I have come a very long way to ask you to solve a simple riddle for me. How can a charcoal maker, such as yourself, who earns only ten cents a day, make enough to live on, pay back a debt, save for his old age, and still have something left over to throw out the window?"

Glancing up from his work at the eager courtier, the charcoal maker slowly shook his head, "Please pardon me, Sir. I am sorry you have made such a long journey, but I can't tell you the answer to the riddle for I have promised not to."

"Hmmm. Yes, of course," smiled the courtier slyly. "But what

do you say to these ten gold pieces?" And he pressed them, one by one, in the charcoal maker's hand.

The charcoal maker looked thoughtfully at the coins but shook his head again, "No, Sir. I really cannot break my promise."

"Well, then, how about this?" demanded the courtier impatiently as he counted out more and more shiny coins.

The charcoal maker picked up each coin and studied it carefully. But still he shook his head, no.

Soon there were one hundred coins in front of him.

"Well, have you anything to say to one hundred?" demanded the courtier.

"Hrrhhumm. Well, you see, Sir," said the charcoal maker as he cleared his throat. "It is very simple. With my earnings I support my family which includes my mother, who took care of me when I was young. Now I am taking care of her. Thus, I am paying back a debt. I also provide for my son, whom I hope will do the same for me when I am old. So, I am saving for my old age. Finally, I must provide a dowry for my daughter, and *that* is as good as throwing money out the window!"

The courtier laughed heartily at the charcoal maker's reply.

"Ah, ha. How very clever. Thank you, my good man, thank you, indeed."

Hastily, he mounted his horse and rode off in the direction of the castle, already picturing himself as First Counsellor of the Kingdom.

That evening when the courtier returned to the castle, the king was seated on his throne by a roaring fire. The courtier boldly approached the king and whispered something in his ear. The king's face suddenly turned bright red with angry surprise.

"So you see, Your Majesty," boasted the courtier in a loud voice, "I have guessed the answer to the riddle and *I* should be made First Counsellor of the Kingdom, as you have promised."

"Yes, yes. I must keep my word, if you did indeed guess the answer to the riddle," replied the disappointed king. "But first I must have a word with the charcoal maker. Have him brought to me at once!"

Before the king had finished his dinner, swift riders brought the charcoal maker to him. Dazzled by the splendor of the castle, the charcoal maker approached the king hesitatingly and bowed.

"Your Majesty, you sent for me?"

"You have broken your promise to me and have told the answer to the riddle!" said the king angrily to the poor charcoal maker. "I thought you were as honest as you were clever. I see now, that this is not so. You deserve to be punished, for dishonesty is the very worst of crimes!"

The charcoal maker stood silently for a few moments and then he spoke out bravely.

"Your Majesty, your anger at me is unjust, for I did exactly as you requested. I did not tell the answer to the riddle until I had seen your Majesty's face one hundred times."

"But that is absolutely impossible!" exploded the king. "You couldn't have!"

"But I did," grinned the charcoal maker, "on each and every one of the hundred coins that the courtier gave to me."

The king looked at the charcoal maker in astonishment, and then burst out laughing, as did everyone in the court.

"Yes, yes you are right. I see that you are even more clever than I thought. And still you kept your promise. I praise you, and curse the courtier in front of the whole court. And I give you three bags of gold. One for your debt, one for your old age, and one to throw out the window."